THE CHARMS OF HONEY CHRONICLES

Vatekia Graves

ABOUT THE AUTHOR

Vatekia is a graduate from Stevenson University. She received her bachelor's degree in Business Information Systems in 2015. Then, she graduated with a Master of Science degree in Business & Technology Management in 2018. Vatekia was a clarinet player in Stevenson University's marching band for 2 years. She participated in the strings and band program as early as the third grade, which was when her love for music began. She was one of the first members of the SU Academic Integrity Committee when it was established. Vatekia has work experience in tutoring, marketing, call centers, hardware repair, and helpdesk roles in not-for-profit and government corporations. Vatekia currently volunteers as a career mentor. Having parents who are in love and married makes a substantial impact on a person's life. Thus, Vatekia is passionate about love; she is also conscious about the reasons of hurt and has liked studying the mind and heart of relationships from a young age.

Vatekia has flourished and, she is determined. Vatekia has a very powerful logical mind, and she can be determined and dynamic in any industry she chooses. She is a great risk taker and a true lover and friend.

Vatekia developed an interest in computers, and she has been passionate about music and writing since she was three years old. Her quick strategic thinking, persistent ways, and troubleshooting ability make her a great technician and goal setter. Writing comes naturally to Vatekia; she writes songs in her free time. She can compose a song or a poem in a few minutes whether it is about love or something random. She loves to go shopping with her family.

Table of Contents

Introduction

This book is a collection of realistic creative poems and stories; various topics such as love, romance, hurt and much more. I want you to explore the wild thoughts, imagine the scenes and navigate through this journey with me.

Stand Up

Stand up Woman...

I said stand

Stand up Man, and be a man

Women, you better fight

With all your might

I am not going to throw a pity party for you

No slaps on the wrist

I don't pay your bills, so I don't have to get that switch off the tree like your parents or ancestors had to do.

Generations are steady changing but one thing remains

We still have power and a voice

Women, you do have a choice

You have the right to hurt him where it hurts you. He hurt you, didn't he? Let his heart hurt too.

Even if that means to walk away and never return

It is better to be alone than to be dumb and repeatedly listening to his lies. Woman, stand up. You hold the power, not the man. All of that labor pain, and you are going to let him talk to you rudely and hit you aggressively like that? Oh, he doesn't mean it. Keep thinking that lady. You must be sick. I am sorry but you are intoxicated with 2000mg of stupid in love lady in the city nearest me. Let me give you some induce vomit medicine so you can vomit it out. This is sad.

Women, don't let me down. Men, treat the ladies right, the children are watching. A real man doesn't need but one woman. If you see a man doing wrong, tell him, in a respectful way. You are the prize. Why do you keep unwrapping yourself? He doesn't deserve such a gift. He hasn't invested his time. Who's to say he isn't lying? That is not your husband yet or will he ever be? Make your own decisions but be wise and think twice. Again, woman, stand up! Don't drop that crown. I would never want to see you frown.

Sitting in my room like dang

Sitting in my room like dang
How can I be so chill?
About how it all went down
The force in my being
The strength of self-control
It is because I believe in the power, the strength, and the
value of people,
I see the dignified defied human stance and the sky
Aluminizing, sophisticated Earth we live on
Not a speck of bad is on the creator
If you have no one else, who will be there to smile with?
Devotion was what kept us
Elegant is as elegant does
If you saw what I saw in you, you would be secure
Or perhaps another bore

Life

He said I am not like other girls. I said I know. I get that
    bread and go to school.
I have a master's degree in technology. Wouldn't you like
    to know?
You know I must hit the store and buy myself a brand-
    new coat.
A coat with some ice, a coat with some shine will be mine
    at the right time.
Drink some tea to soothe my mind. School is not a waste
    of time.
Struggled like a nomad, but now it's my time.
A vanilla smoothie sounds nice at any price while studying
    for this certification.
The sky is the limit, so, I'm going to reach for a million, a
    trillion,
And just pursue this thing called life.
And my mission to begin as
Eager as the Fox that looks for food certain nights
Is my drive for success and my rights
Some people doubted me, but I passed every test,
Society does not care about us blacks, and they don't let
    us rest.
This Coronavirus pandemic is going on
The job market is crazy
National Leaders
Are trying to send us back
To school and work without proper caution, Isn't that
    extreme?
This will bring us under attack,
We must pray to God and trust in his word.
I will take my own advice

For this thing called life
I know everything will be out of sight
So amazing
If I keep chasing my dreams in this thing called life,
I will never give up
The only way is up
I am living my best life
In this thing called life.

How many times?

Yes, I am mad and hurt, but I am learning to get over it. How many times do we have to say, "I am willing to do this for the long term, and I can take the good with the bad"? My mind keeps asking: "Is it normal to go through this many bad situations with someone you love?" "Forget him," it says at times. I wish I didn't give a flying kite, didn't keep caring about someone. But no, I will not care, and you will be all alone. Trust me, no one will put up with your behavior or all of your BS. Even if they do, they can only do it for so long, and it would never last. I love you despite your flaws! I love you more than you will ever know, and you cannot even see that. I have just about had it with you. I mean it! How many freaking times do we go over stuff to make you recognize a good thing when you see one? Yet, your ignorance just forces me to walk away. You have done this often enough for me to notice. You talk about wanting this to work, but you still do things that keep it from working. You have run from your problems often enough for me to notice it. I don't like it at all. You want me to understand. Well, I hope you understand when you get ghosted. Stay, for once. I am beginning to not even care anymore. You don't care, and I don't either. Try dating yourself; try kissing yourself then! Your actions are turning your soul ugly. I hardly recognize you anymore. You can be successful by yourself, but is that any good? So, there it is. Karma will come for you. Then, you will tell me you are missing me, but I don't want to hear it. Miss me with your BS.

Summertime

In the summertime, our love is sweet, like Betty Crocker's
    treats.
In the wintertime, we stick together like glue in the cold. If
    skies are
blue, our love is optimistic—two people dancing in the rain
If thunder rolls, we are blessed to know God's work
We walk in the rain and you give me a covering.
When spring flowers bloom, our love is right,
You drive to my house to pick me up and hold me tight
Letting me know everything will be alright. Our love is
    bold like
fireworks at 11p.m.
When autumn leaves fall, our love is steel
Strong, durable and shining bright like a harvest sun.
From Thanksgiving to Christmas, our love is rising like
    the sun,
Please promise not to run
You going away would not be fun
I might run to the alter to you at our wedding
Wouldn't that be great?
I can't believe we will have a wedding
From season to season our love endures the test of life
I can't wait until the day you are all mine.
You are so fine and truly a gift from above
All the time, we explore and gain new hobbies with strife
That means our love is forever,
I will never leave you ever
In the summertime or any season, I am forever indebted.

You

You make me want to fly to the Florida Keys and around
    the world
So, promise me that you will stay the same always.
In the meantime, I will continue to brighten up your days
More and more can I feel myself growing attached to you.
You are my sexy man and I am your sexy woman
Whatever we must do to be strong, if we ever get weak,
    we will.
You are my creamy caramel latte and I am your tea and
    honey,
But I can be your mocha as well
I can be whatever I dream of,
And I want you to believe that you can be whatever you
    dream of.
If you just put in effort, progress and reach for your goals,
    it takes
patience, but you will do it and I will too.
So, don't be mad at the world for some things not going right,
But rejoice in knowing that I will be by your side
And that I like your company, your warmth, and your soul
So much that I love being wrapped in your arms and I like
    looking at
your curious and calming eyes;
The depths of your eyes show me that you adore me
And that is what I always want to be true in a person.
I want your eyes to stay that way as long as we are suitable
Because you say that I give you hope The other truth is you
    bring so much joy
Into my life and when I think of you I just want more of you,
More of your spirit and more of your laughing spells,
And I am so glad that we met.

The chronicles of whatever

I grew up in a small town where everyone knows everybody. I enjoy the springtime. I have always had a passion for poetry and computers. Ever since I went to college, I have become more open in a mindset way. I have always enjoyed writing creatively. As a kid, I aspired to be a professional clarinetist and singer. However, I feel like songs should have meaning, but people must produce what makes them happy. These rappers make songs about women that are degrading them and in my opinion, twerking is garbage and foolish. If these females keep posting videos of them twerking online, it lets me and everyone else know what kind of person they are, yet they front on social media. It is strange that these same people think that a man wants to marry them when they post pictures with their breasts halfway out talking about they are "on fleek", it's step daddy season, flawless, sexy and all that other unnecessary talk. At the same time, some of these dumb men do marry these whores and try to turn them into housewives and good people and, it doesn't work out. They leave the wholesome women behind and get the easy ones so they can control them and that is a huge problem. Men are quick to like their pictures and videos and even comment giving them the attention they want which is pathetic as well. What is wrong with this world? We need God now more than ever. Stop saying men are dogs! Men are hunters. They might take all they can take as long as you give it. I am sorry you did not get the attention you needed as a kid, so you get all the attention now on social media and in your bed by men: how cute, I mean yuck. That sort of behavior is not funny: it is sad and a disgrace. Men and women need to wake up. Do you see a future with someone who acts provocative online to the world? Where is their self-respect? Where are their tiaras, the locks, and the keys? It is time to make changes if you want to see changes in your next relationships. If your parents were not examples, maybe a friend can be an example. Well just wanting better should be motivation as well. Don't get comfortable just living and feeling empty. The chronicles of whatever is whatever the case may be, whatever the people do will cease and a resolution will come soon if they work for it. The chronicles of whatever consist of no matter what happens in life, I will always be okay because I know God. He is a miracle worker. No matter what, I will always push to see the next day whether it is dark or cloudy. Some of these new rappers are ruthless and odd. 2020 was a nightmare, and now it is 2026 and people rap about sex, drugs, and weed; how pathetic! Why can't they rap about something meaningful? Isn't life more than a substance?

However, everyone will not like everything that you do anyway. There will always be haters or opinions. If you need help, get help and stop abusing illegal drugs. If you can do better, put in work, and act like you know you are capable. Stop blaming others for your problems. The world is not okay right now.

Love

I do not have any reason to see another man. I know who my heart wants. I know who will care for me through life's' ups and downs. I know who I want. I know who I feel safe and protected near. I always knew but, now I feel even more ready. If he said, let's get married in 2 weeks, I would be all for it. With no hesitation, no crazy thoughts, no asking why, no feeling scared, no uneasiness. It may sound crazy to you, but I would do it because that's what you do for love and your happiness. He doesn't even know how many lives he touches with his smile. The impact is unforgettable. In relationships, you must give and take with your partner. Well, I will try to give all I can give if he is reciprocating it back. I will take all I can take as well. He appreciates a classy, sassy woman when he sees her. I am thankful for a strong man. He loves to be in my arms, and I love to be in his. He is my king. I am his queen. I know he loves me because his tone changes when he speaks to me, his face lights up, his eyes get brighter when he sees me. I don't have to worry when he is away because he always checks in to make sure I am okay. He is my man. He is my supporter, my heart, my soul, my best friend, my inspiration, and my life partner. He is my strawberry smoothie with a chilled sandwich to match. I love him with all my heart. He makes my heart smile when I wake up in the morning next to him. He always knows what to say, how to say it, and what to do to make me invigorated. He brings me breakfast in bed often to let me know he cares. If he oversleeps, he still makes sure I get fed. He is a blessing to my life. I want to explore more hobbies because I have a journey partner now in him. Of course, he makes me mad as well. However, I can never stay mad at him for long. We always communicate and work out our problems. I am vulnerable to him. When you love someone, you don't let the past define your future. He trusts me and wants me and only me. Sadly, some people will never experience true love because of pride. I have dealt with pride issues in the past. However, I realized that why live life not going after what you want. If you can't be vulnerable with your husband, wife, girlfriend, or boyfriend, you have a problem to fix. It is wise to break barriers and let your partner see the real you. You should not visit your homeboys every day when your wife is home worried about you, not knowing if you are okay or not. She has a reason why she feels unappreciated. Stop saying she is overreacting. Put yourself in her shoes. You think about what your children, husband, or wife wants before you go out with your friends when you are in a relationship. It seems simple, but you would be surprised to see how many people would be clueless about this. They say I am not used to telling someone where I am going and checking in with them every so often. If they want a woman, they should learn to work for the relationship and make changes. If a man truly wants you, he will do everything to get you and keep you no matter the drive or circumstance. We have options. If he treats you like an option, say call me when you grow up and learn some sense. You hold the sovereignty so, act like it. When the person is right for you, you will know. You will feel it in your spirit when you meet the right one for you. My lover and I finish each other's sentences many times. You won't have to ask; how do you know when you have found the right one.

Yeah, Yeah, Yeah, Yeah

Our love can stand the test of time
I really like you
I think I am falling in love with you
You are so funny but serious too
You make me laugh like no other.
Yeah, Yeah, Yeah, Yeah
You made me trust like no other I believe what you say and
Don't have to doubt anything.
I have a clear mind,
I make logical decisions
I pray for you
You pray for me
We both seek God and praise him
That's a big plus
We can talk for a long time and be so comfortable about
anything.

Our Love

My love for you is endless
As certain as there is an ocean
A wave like the wind flows.

The way I am attracted to you is amazing
By holding each other with deep intimacy
Your hand I will hold as I kiss you and massage you.

No ocean will be too far for me to reach you
Our love is like a silver magnet always reflecting and being
    relevant.
My love for you is endless As certain as there is a God,
The way I am attracted to you is amazing.

Your hand I will hold as I journey with you
No ocean will be too far for me to reach you
Our love is like a movie always in sync and being relevant.

I would walk ten miles if I had to
Just to feel secure
And to make you secure;

This is not a game But we are winning
I scored when I found you
Let's be about making experiences
When you were down
I was your rock you see,

I needed a rock A long time ago
It was when I found you, I believe.
There was a change

An undeniable sense of knowing
That you were meant to be

In my life exactly
No matter how mad I was at you
My heart had a spot for you.
You realized that when you were in trouble
A ride or die, a real MVP
Describes me as your queen.

I saw something in you
That I wanted you to see in yourself
You didn't love yourself

I could see right through your soul from your eyes without
        even seeing your face from a picture I saw your face.

Yet I saw deep, deep pain in your eyes
I saw hurt; I saw a broken heart
It needed repair
You said your parents weren't together as you grew up
Well, that makes three reasons You were lost, cold, and
        confused
I remember that day
When fate was established
A larger thirst was gained in us
You said that faithful day you will remember

I'm Trying

I am trying to act like I don't want you
I am trying to think of negative things about why it
    wouldn't work
out, but I shouldn't
There are no red flags, but I keep trying to think of reasons
The only thing I can think of is that he is not financially
    stable, yet he
has a job
I just need to chill and see what happens
He is funny, cool
I'm trying not to do certain things but
He just has me laughing a lot and I can't resist.
His smile, his laugh
It's like he is someone I can tell my problems to and he
    listens
It's like he understands me in a way:
He likes independence like I do
He wants to spread his wings like I do
He likes quietness and calmness.
I should give him a shot
He hasn't lied as far as I know
I just wish he was in college too
He used to be
Babe, I want to talk to you, but I can't pressure anyone.
Lol
I'm trying to be someone you can trust
I'm trying to be someone you can tell your problems to
    more often
I'm trying to be your only one
I'm trying to be the one you call during the day and night.
I like you

I know that you know that
I guess you think that since you aren't completely estab-
    lished, you
shouldn't date.
Well it is the truth
I need to get through school first anyway
So, I can be okay with that I'm trying.

Honor of Spring

My magnificent Spring
Grace me with your light
You inspire me to write
How I hate the way you move and come to a halt
Invading my mind all day and night is love
Always dreaming about the warmth of your essence
Let me compare you to the sound of a harp being played
You are more perfect, meaningful, and evident
Force clouds through the universe and revitalize the preg-
    nant tulips
Springtime has the elegance perfectly blended
How do I hate you? Let me count the ways
My allergies ascend
I hate your heat
Thinking of the joy of how you fill my days
Now I must walk away with a scorned heart
Never have I felt so much peace
Remember my beam because of you while we are apart.

Having fun tonight

I feel like having fun tonight
The sky looks so beautiful
I see the lights flashing
And baby, I am for taking chances.
I will do as I please
As the sky gets darker
Let's have some fun all day but especially tonight
Maybe romance is in the air
You have a warm embrace
I felt it
I feel right at home
The way your hair lays a certain way
You know what you are doing
The best part is about to start
That look in your eyes and I feel like having fun tonight
Last night, you were the one I was missing
But today you are standing right
there;
I think I may have found my future in this: I am all for tak-
    ing chances.
Let's start with some candlelight
Oh yea,
Turn the lights off.

Flowing Energy

I want to love you, every night every day
You know I love our laughs
I want you in my life, every night, and every day.
You are the reason for some of my smiles, it is a feeling I
      get when I
see a text from you
Do you know that?
I want to love you, every night, every day.
I hope I am the one you are thinking of
I think about you every night and morning I think I am
      falling for you.
Stay here with me for a while
Let's chill
I will be your support
Just keep me laughing.

Her thoughts of him

Terra gets on with life with skill and as a sexy minded person.
And with a dreamboat
He likes basketball, and he likes relaxing.
She likes to contemplate nice behavior.
But when she starts to daydream,
Her mind turns straight to how sweet he is.
Sometimes, she looks at herself and into his eyes,
And she knows he means what he says
I notice the way she thinks about him with a smile,
Soft lips she just can't resist.
Their bodies are in sync when they touch so softly
Being in his arms feels safe and cozy,
But she thinks his nice personality
His cool ways making her life fun.
Why is it so charming?
Nice personality or...
Sweet? She likes to use words like "awesome"
To describe the way, her husband is in the bedroom and
    outside;
She likes to use words like "good" as she should
Shouldn't being with him feel exciting?

IDK anymore

My love is so real but maybe yours isn't anymore.
Why do we keep going through it?
I want this to work yet it must get better.
I know that every relationship has ups and downs
I am willing to go through ups and downs
We have been through a lot already.
We are supposed to be a team
But you aren't acting like a team player
So, I made the choice of forgetting you
Maybe you will come around
And maybe you will not
The depths of my soul you touch
I feel that you love me dear I know I love you.

Your parents did not work out
So that is why you work at us too
You want to love but don't know how
Eager to open but you resist.
Sure, you want to like two birds kiss
A dove is pretty and rare
Why can't love be fair?
Idk anymore
You have become rotten
You let me freshen you, but
You are rotten again
You are unsure that you are qualified, but you are still so
    loveable.

My exes were insane

His love that wasn't true
See how blind we can be
My ex was insane
Well I wasn't blind; I just didn't want to see things
　　　sometimes.
I want to see the good in people
My future husband would not act in such ignorance or
　　　disgust
I finally let you go for good
You are bad news
The way you screamed was insane
You better release your stress in a positive way
No one wants a lover who is crazy in the head.

Misery loves company,
But I don't want to be your company anymore
It was good while it lasted
You want company because your love is not true
You said you are a better you when I am with you:
That is a lie,
You will not change.
Wanting revenge on family is wrong
Wanting someone to love is wrong when you aren't whole
They can't fill your void You have deep issues
Don't tell me I am mean.

You have no room to speak words to me
You are not a trustworthy person I show tough love
Can't take the punch?
Then be gone
Wait a minute! I blocked you!

Clearing your mind is what you should do!
Bottled up emotions are not good
Release them before it controls your mind
Never mind you already lost your mind
That day the way you screamed was insane
I don't care if I ever see you again
You acted possessed, but you can't see that you are blessed.

One guy acted like he thought he was God
and was controlling because he was mad about some-
    thing dumb.
Not on my watch, not on this Earth, no man or woman will
    run me.
I was saying, you must have lost your mind, who do you
    think you are?
You aren't God and, you will never be God. You don't know
    what I will do. That is not even all of it: I dumped him
    the next day.

He cried like a baby on the phone when I left him and, I
did not care. I hung up and, you need to do the same. Stop
answering their calls! Block toxic females and males. No
more! No tears, no frowns, no more pain. People be careful
who you date before you get too serious. Some men will lie
so much and, it is pathetic. One guy lied about food before,
so you know if you lie about small things: you will lie about
everything. Watch out for the red flags! The point of this
poem is to give advice and to know what to look out for. Do
not accept poor behavior and watch out for patterns.

What I like

I get on with life as a hard worker
Steady chasing goals
I'm a smart person
I like basketball on Saturdays,
I like running while playing duck duck goose
I like to contemplate ideas,
But when I start to daydream,
My mind turns straight to money and my goals.
Sometimes I look at myself and I look into my eyes
Through a mirror
I notice the way I think about money with a smile
Curved lips I just can't disguise,
But I think the drive is making my life worthwhile.
Why is it so hard for me to decide which I love more?
Silver or...
Money?
Shoes or clothes?
Gadgets or glitter?
I like to use words like ice and fire
I like to use words like awesome
I like to use words about characters, but when I stop my
    discussion.
My mind turns straight to money and a house
Sometimes I look at myself and I look into my eyes
I notice the way I think about money with a smile
Curved lips I just can't disguise,
But I think its zest making my life worthwhile
Why is it so hard for me to decide which I love more?
Music or...
Money?

I like to hang out with my nephew and family
I like to kick back with my loves, but when left alone,
My mind turns straight to money
Sometimes I look at myself and I look into my eyes
I notice the way I think about money with a smile
A big house with some dogs
Curved lips I just can't disguise
But I think its music making my life worthwhile
Why is it so hard for me to decide which I love more?
Music or...
Money?
I'm not too fond of phony people
Smiling to your face and talking behind your back
Say it to my face, you freak,
I really hate thieves
But I just think back to money and love
And I'm happy once again.

To think we used to be so close

To think we used to be so close and now look at us. We aren't even talking since yesterday. Sad but true. I don't want to hear any excuses. Just leave me alone. I will never forget anything, but I learned to never trust anyone. Even if we fix it, I will never forget the pain, the conversations, the way we once felt. The way we talked about our future. Maybe that is over too. I want you but then again, I don't know. I deserve love but is that with you? Who will love you despite your flaws besides God? But I love you that much. It may not even ever go away. You just don't understand the depth of my love. I just can't keep on dealing with these types of problems. I have enough problems of my own. I was willing to fix it. I was willing to do whatever it takes so that I could be happy as well as you. I was willing to do whatever it takes just to see you. Yet, you just put stuff to a halt. You know what my goals have been and what will likely happen.

You cannot have your cake and eat it too. Something has got to give. I understand your dreams and such, but you are living like you don't care about anyone but yourself. Don't you want someone by your side when the tough times come, someone to go through the good and the bad experiences with? You must care about others to grow as a person. You can't live in this world all alone. I am not saying that we must last but we can at least get along and be friends or nothing at all. You can't keep doing things to hurt me; it is not fair to me.

We have been through so much in a way. It seems to be like all you do to me is love me, hurt me, and back and forth.

I can't keep giving you my energy and you are not putting it to good use. We were doing well lately until now. Be wise and learn from the past and from the present. Every time you are inconsiderate, all you do is make it easier for me to live without you.

What do you really want? You will be surprised when you stop getting responses from me. All you do is talk sweet nothing's and it doesn't align with any actions. Keep saying what you are going to do. What good is that? It is bullshit. You keep talking about dreams that will never come true unless you make it happen. This is not a dream. This is the reality of life. Saying I want to do this and that. For what? You must want to be single so I will remove myself. You don't make me a priority but claim I am your rock etc. That's foolish. Out of all the options I have the only person I want is you. You are too blind to see that. I have given you so much of my energy and it is all in vain. It is not fair to me. I am not giving you anymore of my time for nothing. No one can get their precious time back. I know that I love you, but you don't seem to care. It is like cooking, turning the stove off and, never putting the food away in the refrigerator. It gets old and time dies.

I care about you

I care so much
Baby, you mean so much to me. I feel like we are right for
    each other,
I want you with me.
I want "us" forever
I believe we can make it work
If you are faithful to me and vice versa.
I hope you will stay true to me because I am being real with
    you. I
don't have time for games or lies, No bullshit and I hate
    drama.
I want to be your forever love.
I don't want to have to be skeptical, etc. And, I don't want
    you to be
skeptical. And I remember what people tell me
I remember a lot; I want to get to know you.
I also feel like we have come a long way, and I want us
    to last.
Remember: I am always here for you, whether you want to
    talk, cry,
anything.
I feel in my heart that we can make it last forever.
I believe we are meant to be.
I want to do everything with you.
I want to kiss you, learn with you,
To be happy and in love with you, my future husband,
    share awesome
experiences with you;
Sing with you, and make videos together
I want to hold you
So just hold on and don't let go

I want to be with you through thick and thin
This is for real
Believe that.
Do you remember the first time we separated?
I was sad and felt like I had a heart attack.
I never cried so much. It was awful.
I couldn't get contented. I never had that happen before.
    That's
another reason why I believe you are the one. I can't live
    without you.
I need you baby, well, I want you.

Missing him

I can't wait to hold you in my arms
Love you forever, my baby.
I love you so deep
I miss you
I want to cry
You are my companion
I miss him
He is so special to me
He has me wanting to get married soon
Because I know he is the one for me
I want to give him all my love I feel like I need him
I can't live without him.
He is my other half. I want him here with me. I will love you
    forever.
I want to have your children
I am so ready to give you all of me
When I look into your eyes, it will be amazing
I already know
You are my sexy love, so sexy
I love him
You make me want to take that dive
I can never say goodbye baby,
You are the only man I want in this world.
And there are lots of men, but you are the only important
    one I want
So, my knight in Shining Armor, don't worry I will take care
    of you.
All you need is God and my love, and you will be set.
You have me wanting to do things that people dream of
I love being with you. Last night, I felt your presence. I told
    you I love you.

Love is patient, love is kind...take love slowly
But since we are sure of our love, we can take it at our
     speed. If we
fight, please don't ever go to bed mad at me; talk to me, tell
     me how
you feel, love me
Because tomorrow is not promised for us humans
We are a team
We must stick together
We can work anything out.

No strings attached

You want to obtain something with no strings attached
And there is no right or wrong way to get it
Utilitarianism is the principle of we learn from the consequences
You think you are slick, but I can read between the lines.
There are different ways to manage ethical behavior
An organization can have a code of contact
Provide proper training,
But you can't teach new tricks to someone set in their ways,
Some old people think they know everything because they
    are older.
Did you see when the sky was made? No.
Did they make highways? No.
Receiving unsolicited e-mails concerning special offers
Emails that says someone is poor in Africa and a King
Or emails
Asking for confidential information to win an iPhone is very
    unethical
A guy asked her for $50 for a new hair cut on their first date
She better tell him Adios
So bold, so cold
His eyes were his soul
I think he could play a good role
She said no about the $50 he asked for and that she needs
    $50 for
her hair and toes
Oh, and her bows
Many people were not raised right
I noticed that as I began dating
I wouldn't mind waiting
For a love that's true.
Many males think they are gold He must be 70% gold

Not the 100% that is true
So deceptive, scheming, and loose
But displaying as a Dove
Fronting for the gram Fronting for their FAM Until some-
     one says bam
I would rather eat spam You act like a hound
Your nose trouble is out of hand.
That's all folks,
Or should I give you another round? He is nowhere to
     be found
Because I turned him down.
You may hear lies You may hear rumors
He says bad things because he can't talk to me
He can't get his way
He is lame
So, he puts disrespect on my name
What a shame!
I do not want anything to be loose like his pants.
He said," he can put me in a trance".
He does not even have a chance
I want to make a mark on what I want to claim
No more games
I am not to blame

You grace me with your presence

When you come around, a smile forms on my face
Bright as the summer is my reflection
Your perseverance is enduring from day to day.
Please keep haters at bay
They creep back in like a thief in the day or night
They shoot in broad daylight and even put up a good fight.
Twisted as the string on the artwork in the car
Deceptive but bold whether close or afar
Didn't your mom teach you to do no wrong?
Maybe they were raised by stray cats or perhaps a drug
    abuser
Always picking up scraps in someone's back or front yard
Until the alarm sounds, all hands-on deck
The audacity of them to take hard earned possessions
Now they will remember that session
Now they missed their blessing
Next time they will grace me with presence
Elegance, diligence, and not deception.

Love is blind

Wow, she was so wrong, How can she do that?
She saw his smile that was so very bright, but he was in a
    disguise.
How can she choose to date him when he has anger issues?
She looked beyond his flaws until it progressed;
Love is blind so using your brain and not your heart is
    best. `
She is crazy beautiful Beautiful is as beautiful does
Fancy is as fancy does and fancy flaunts
When the creator is watching from above
A tranquil, optimistic spirit indebted in the truth and root
The constant urge to go above and beyond the distant
    shores where
peace originated is where she seeks to be?
A fractured knee but she walks like a lioness:
Invincible and poise,
While the eagle lurks eyes gigantic raging like fire and his
    beak is
a yellow sword his wings expand sure as a full moon
    captivating?
Every scene eager for its retreat to devour until then he sits
    high as
the mountain top.

Roses

I think when I see you it will be Roses
Every time at first sight
Will be like explosions of gratitude
Whether near or far there will be romantic candlelight
Probably in your eyes
Probably in my eyes
Let it be our guide
Let's take this on a ride
Captivating our souls and devotion
God said put us together
For he knew this was far better than our past endeavors.
We cherish the moments we have
We can't deny the feeling
I love you beyond the shorelines
We made a choice to reunite
We made a choice to rekindle our love
This choice has been spectacular
This choice
I would choose you over our favorite ice cream, Cookies
    n' Cream
If I could have anything in this world, it would be you
I would still choose you if it was between seeing you and a
    celebrity.
You show me every day why I am your wife
You show me every day the man I fell in love with
Because we fit
You are a part of my dreams
A part of my soul
A feeling that I never had with anyone else ever
A feeling that never goes away even if I wanted it to

It remains
Captivating, calming, energizing, and romantic
Is our passion for each other
Strong, flowing, beautiful, and irresistible breathtaking
Because our love is like roses
Because my lover, what we have is roses.

Scorns of the heart

Simon hates your guts
Well, you made him feel unheard;
You never wanted to even hear the response.
He tried to help you.
And he did not comprehend
So, you called him simple minded
He lacked some common sense, yet he was brilliant
    every time.
Simon created a hit song and won an award
The sunset and he was sad
His dad name called yet he wasn't fair
Simon was a prince suffering from verbal abuse but not
    physical.
Why do people not think before they speak?
The son thought to himself
I will end my life tonight
He won't have to worry about me anymore
No one cares for me anyway
If he thinks I am crazy, he may be delusional though
The son noticed as time went on, he became wealthier and
    capable
of learning
Things that were not up his alley
I met this girl at school. She said she feels like she is living
    in a jail
with family; With family;
Aren't families supposed to be kind?
"The same with friends, teachers, just people in general
When I started dating I realized
Strangers are nicer sometimes and they don't even know you

Isn't that bologna? Why is this true?
Life is short. Why spend so much time being mad for silly
    reasons?"
They always complain
Acting like they don't know God But praise his name at
    church Why don't I just leave them behind? Crying out
    to God,
He said, "I will give you peace for I am the vine".
The son told his dad no one can be good at everything
The dad said, "You are right, I am sorry."
"Why are you so harsh?"
Simon's father said, "I need to do better and today I will
    start it;
Every day he would get mad and call me that Today, I will
    bury the generational curse,
I am so sorry for what I did to you."
Simon said: You can be sorry all you want but the pain is
    still there
but some day it will be better.
You see,
When you called me those things? You made me feel worthless,
I even thought about ending it all
I went inside the cabinet and had 10 pills in my hand
And just held them until they melted.
I was going to take them, but Rebecca called and said she
    loved me
and couldn't wait to see me next week.
I stopped from ending my life because Joseph texted me
    and said I
had a brilliant work idea
And how nice I am at work and that I made his work day
    great when
he sees me
Because I felt like you used to be a strong role model to me
They stopped as I got older
You are not perfect so you should not have looked
    down on me

My scars are down inside, and you cannot see
My wounds are dark near my heart and sometimes I don't
    want it to beat
Be nice, be kind, and remember what you do will follow you.
So, no, I do not want to talk to you
Not ever you see
Because I lost a friend in you
So, I continue to smile because someone else is far worse
    than me
No one called them to reassure them that they were needed
Their families were not so lucky
Their son died and I saw their stories on the news
You see I will love and treat my kids nicely with patience
Whether I am mad or not
I will not have a bad temper
I will smile at them and call them beautiful because you
    did not call
me that.
Kids don't ask to be born
So, don't say I would not have to do this if it wasn't for you,
You created me; I am a gift from God
Don't say that I am a nuisance I am the son of the Most High
I will give them what I longed for and so will my wife
I will be the best parent ever
The quote is sticks and stones may break my bones, but
    words will
never break me. You see, that is not true
Being called a word hurts far worse than stones and sticks
    hitting
against my flesh
Be patient, be gentle, be trusting, and always show love.
This is not a game
This is life
I wish you had changed I wish you were nice
I wish you were considerate;
You are toxic even if we share the same name
I am sorry your dad was like that too,

But I am not to blame
I do not want to be associated with you ever.
I met a man and he told me to forget you
Ever since I did, you see I won a million dollars
I am moving away
You might not see me again I am freeing my mind.
Sometimes I wished I was not adopted
I was cold, lonely but happy
A child with a yearning heart of love
But you failed me
I think you are the scum of the Earth;
Is it fair to raise a child or adopt a child and abuse him?
Why have kids if you will insult them?
Why look down on them?
Maybe your parents looked down and frowned at you
The pain I endured did not have to be true
Maybe I just wanted a hug or a kind gesture
You don't know what was on my mind
Because of you I felt as though you were against me
Because of you I have a hole in my heart
Because of you I am another man scorned
Because of you I lost hope
I did not have a father,
You were more like an evil relative
Sad like someone receiving a broken toy in the mail,
Yet I smiled every chance I got
My smile was so bright it could light up a room but when
     I got behind
closed doors, I cried in his room. Parents, stop belittling
     your kids
Don't watch them get teased and not react,
Listen to how their school day went
They don't want to talk to you Because you are rude and
     judgmental
Enrich your kids' lives no matter how old they are
They are smart, courageous, and seek trust and approval;
They can show love if they are shown love

Be who you want them to look up to
If they sense disapproval, their hearts are bruised at any
     age just
like you can bruise anyone else.
My therapist said that I have issues with trust because
     of you
So, kudos for the best dad award
I wish it was true Karma will bite you This is true
The pain you caused is for a lifetime
Words have power
Speak nice words, not horrific words
So, please be kind to everyone you encounter
You never know what someone is going through.
Send a kind note He hated your guts
Well, you made him feel unheard.
I heard that a man jumped from a bridge last night, On
     New Year's,
Next time it might be you!

Don't trust these dudes

Asking when am I coming up there,
I told you I am not
That is irrelevant
Messages deleted
No reply
I bet he learned his lesson
You never know
Dudes aren't worth a dime is true to some regard.
He can have a girlfriend, fiancé, or wife
And still say he never loved her
He does not want her
He always wanted you
Don't trust these dudes,
They don't follow the rules
They will leave you confused
Have your heart feeling bruised
Tell lies to your face, Isn't that a disguise?
Don't tell me I overreact; I will hit you with this bat.
They don't love you
Don't fall for the hype.
Listen to your gut,
Use your brain,
Girls just want to have fun but only if it is the right one

Evil thoughts and memories

Why did you let this happen? I see a shadow in the tub
    Your bf hates me
Is it him?
He comes in at night and pretends to be you at first
He makes me perform things
I should not do and that I don't want to ever see
He tells me to be quiet and not say a word,
I obey and he continues putting it in without words,
Eva be quiet, just take it Until it hurts and I push away
You ask why I am single. It is because of your bf; I really
    liked guys, but
I don't feel safe around them anymore
When any man comes close, my skin itches, and I get stiff
    and feel sad
My mind takes over me
My heart feels weak, but it still beats steady.
Plague evil demanding thoughts form in my head
My ex-bf wanted a hug and I pushed him away,
I always think of the way your bf did that
Your bf held me, your bf brushed my hair just to be closer
    to me and you let him.
As soon as you left for work, he approached me every day
His long shaft on my leg felt like a coffee cup
His skin felt like summer:
Sticky but scorching and sparkling.
Why didn't you know?
You were supposed to be my protector
You needed to pay attention to me more often;
Your bf got me pregnant
I am sorry, mom, But it is your fault
I am only 11, just a pre-teen What should I do?

Kids aren't supposed to be pregnant.
I contemplated suicide but I love my baby too much
I will pay attention to my child, mom.
Mom, I need your support
Can we start over?
First, get rid of your bf before this is over
Mom, I love you,
I forgive you
This is your grandchild.
I want him/her to know you
My children won't be followed at night
I will turn on the night light and make sure of it
I will protect them at all costs
If I ever date again, they will go to work with me if they must
If I must use the bathroom, they will sit by the door and
     wait for me
This is crazy
I must live in fear,
Sometimes I feel like I want to jump off a pier
I won't leave them home with my bf like you did
I am concerned
This new way of life must be learned.

<u>She told me</u>

Hello! Are you looking for your daughter?
When you threw the TV against the wall
The glass hit her back and messed up her spine and her
    chest is
bruised;
She has a dent in her back and a horrific scar on her chest
She had about five surgeries to try to fix it.
However, each time they gave her medicine that didn't
    work well,
She gained 100 lbs. from recovery
She is in so much pain she said it feels like a bowling ball
    is on her
back as she walks.
Her walk is crippling
Do you remember when you told her she looks like she is
    100 years
old when she walks?
How dare you be so cruel?
You tried to ruin her, but she gained strength
Her back is swollen in the middle like a beaver's tail
You told her she was beautiful when she was a teenager
    and went to prom
Now, you call her a fat donkey
She even told me you even tried to sell her to a drug dealer
    for $800.
You should be locked up
I already called Child Protective Services on you
I am her therapist.
Please come to my office tomorrow ASAP,
You owe her an apology
She said she had so much pain in her heart and eyes

Are red like ketchup
She said you were her best friend Now she said you call her
     a whore
She said she had sex with two men at once yesterday to
     make her feel beautiful
She cries to God, but he never answers,
But I told her that I am bringing the pastor next week here
     to pray for her
I hope you know she said she felt like trash
You were supposed to be a single mom and you did not
     work half time.
Your daughter is pregnant. She showed me the results.
She said she doesn't know who her child's father is
Because she was drunk and had unprotected sex over 50
     times last year.
I am glad she doesn't have any diseases.
She said she felt like she had a mind disease that started
     in her teens.
I told her it was called mental illness.
She doesn't know how to spell well because you told her
     she was
dumb and stopped teaching her when she was 12.
I am writing this to you because I am concerned about you.
Tell me what is on your mind. Please come see me tomorrow.
Her time is valuable and so is yours. PS.
When she ran away,
I found her on the street. She lives with me at my house.

Gifts

In the Bible, Proverbs 18:16 states that "A man's gift maketh room for him and, brings him before great men." I heard Steve Harvey say that on a TV show before and it stuck with me. So, I looked it up and thought about that. I realized that I have always had a passion for creative writing so why not pursue it? Nothing is holding me back. The world should hear my expressions, my pain, my joy, and feel my vibe. The world needs to know that God can keep you from falling no matter what comes your way. Yes, you may cry, you may be on your death bed, but Jesus is able. If he can heal the blind man and make him see, just imagine what he can do for you. Trust and believe his word. In all your ways acknowledge him and he will direct your path. Some of us don't read like we should but make it a priority because we may be living in the last days. We need to put on the whole armor of God so that we may be able to withstand temptation and sickness. "When you feel yourself getting a scratchy throat, rebuke it and say "I am healed in Jesus name. I believe I am taking healing." If you truly believe what you say and have faith, you will stop the illness."

Love you down

Going back and forth, what are we doing?
If anybody's got you, it's me
I want to show how much I love you
So, let me love you
I want to be the one to know you; I want to be
The one to show you
I want to be the one to give you what you need
I am trying to love you down
I got that good love
Baby
I want to be
The one you call
I want to be the one in your dreams
I am trying to be the one you yearn for
I want to be the one to have that effect on you
You know what I am talking about
You need to be loved, loved, loved

Nepotism

Nepotism is a controversial issue
Nepotism is when employers only seem to hire family mem-
    bers or
people that they already know.
Nepotism
Is a cruel ethical issue
Which needs to be stopped
Nepotism
It still exists just like racism
We can all decide what is right for ourselves. Nepotism
demonstrates the concept of relativism: If they don't sup-
    port me, I
will not support them.
My hope is that nepotism is diminished
Nepotism
Still remains a division amongst us

Our dreams

Give birth to your visions Give birth to your dreams
You loved me when I had nothing
I loved you when you had nothing
You loved me when I was poor
For that, I love you far more than honey
And now that I am rich, I do this all for us
And I am yours forever
You were there to cry with me You were there to pray for me
       We pray together We laugh together We rap together
I gave birth to our thoughts
Our dreams are unfolding right in front of our curious eyes
Jealous people wanted to see us fold
But we are very bold
Bold in our careers, characters and in our styles
We are blossoming through every strife
Like the flames in the fireplace that heat the room
Like the fire in their eyes when we walk in a room
Like the cat purring on the 3-tier toy
Like the scorching summer and breeze before a storm
We went on a plane together
We soared above the horizon
You accompanied me to the store
I bought a pair of Adidas shoes in black
Yet you said they were fire
See, before our success, we confided in each other
There wasn't a dry eye there at our party
The alliteration of our rhymes Oh we are so spontaneous!
Displaying our agony and triumph in the way we spoke
This goes to show
We are no joke even though we took a major blow
A tranquil yet astonishing scene

Now, we are living our dreams.
There is no place nor position I'd rather be
Giving birth to our dreams
Is what I will do forever I have us forever
I will help you break open the hinderance of the mold
And let the aroma of your fragrance take me under a spell
Please don't make me yell
Our secrets and dreams I won't tell
If I smell a rat, best believe I will support you in ending
     their plan and bet
My mission will be to build our empire and keep predators
     at bay
I gave birth to our dreams
I would not have it any other way

Pain

You heard the tears
You heard the melancholy cries
You heard the frustration in my voice
You knew the nervousness in my racing mind
Yet you gave me a stunning present Even though you expe-
    rienced trauma
A rough life left you confused, unsure of your next move
I thought you wanted more out of life
That is what we both wanted; we agreed to that
You said, "What is success if I don't have anyone to share
    it with?"
And gave me words of peace and joy
You remained the same Until I saw a pattern Pain
Before I knew it, I was believing your sugar-coated lies
You said you wouldn't be like my past You painted a pic-
    ture of our life together
You distorted that peaceful image You gave me a motive
    for doubt
Pain
A person walked right over my heart
And placed an opaque fox there to rest
A person who told me their dreams
A person who gave me their devotion
A person who calmed my spirit Whether in pain or moping
A person whom I gave a reason to smile to
Why must you ask?
How can a person be filled with so much pain?
Bitter like sauerkraut cooked with vinegar
His voice was satisfying like a harp
You could not hear hurt But it was in his eyes
Every smooth and melodious rift told a story

The stretch of his vocabulary was innocent
Of the conniving trip that awaited them
The aching of my heart was equivalent to a tremor from an
    acute ear
infection
Pounding, aching, hearing sounds I didn't want to
The pauses of pain were replaced with caring expressions
I feel as though I had run for two hours without a break
You closed the window though my fingers were in sight
The indignation of my fingers; oh, the shock in my upper body!
You wiped every heavenly thought away and left a
    black cloud
To rain over my head
I would have done anything just to keep us happy
The glass globe I made for you has now been thrown out
    the window
Broken just like my heart Shattered glass particles
I evacuated you from my mind
My head swam with poison, yet it managed to flow; my
    voice was
great but now you move a current that produces decoding
Every time I speak about you to friends
My back feels warm like the sun beaming on a car
Eyes feel heavy and they hurt from crying; I imagine you
    plucking
them for hours
I gave you hope, love, and joy
And this is what I receive in return
A musician with a broken string is not eager to perform in
    front of a crowd
Well, I wanted more fun times, not pain

We were made for each other

We were made for each other
I was made to be the one you love
I was made to be the one you smile at
I was made to be your treasure
I was made to go through the struggle with you
I was made to go through the rain with you
I was made to go through the storm with you
I could find a million reasons why I am yours
And I am yours
You are my devotion
We are so in sync with each other
We are made for each other
I am waiting for the day when we will fatefully meet again
All this time we have been talking All this time we have
    been flirting
I can't think of a life without you
Because we have been close since I was a young adult
You were mentally a boy
Now, you are a grown man and you know what you want
We always desired love
We parted ways but never truly My mind was always on you
I know this is true
We had to go through certain past lovers and experiences
    to grow
To mold, adapt to change, learn what love consisted of
Because, my love,
We were made for each other

First or thirst?

The first time I saw your face
I felt like I was in a race; my heart skipped a beat
You said, "Do you want to take a seat?"
My mind couldn't stay still
I was in a maze, in deep thought of all the different ways I
        could.
Dance
Sit...never mind
It wouldn't be PG
This is our first date
I will tell you later
My wish is your command
You want me to be happy
Even if my hair is nappy
Confident in my walk
Sassy is the way I talk
My thighs touch like glue
I bet you could sing the blues
Because you aren't getting anything from me
But the news
Compliments on your shoes
A smile when I am mad to make you confused; do my hips
        entice you?
Do you wonder if my lips feel like sizzling butter?
I bet you wish you knew
If only you knew my thoughts
If only you knew my song
You would want to take me home too
Energy flowing in my mind, a twinkling in your eyes
Eyes bright, they are my sonnet to you
You may look with all your might

Oh no! I am not letting you take a bite
The rhythm in my step is the way I would count when I
    touch your ear
And whisper sweet nothings
To make you wonder
As I close the door
Leaving you hungry and begging for more

Magnet

There is a magnet between us
I feel the pulling of our beings—don't you feel that?
A force that can't be seen but felt
I can read your mind
I heard what you said
I was about to say that too I add to your sentences Exactly,
     yes, that is true All you want is a listening ear
All you want is a gentle embrace
Your lungs are weak from weeping too many days
There are so many things
I want to enhance and articulate
And count the ways
I enjoy my days
You stimulate the fibers of my veins
My mind is crowded with clouds at thought of you
You are the crusade of my heart and, your stance
Makes me blush
Ever since you came into my world
I have been glad to be your girl
There is a magnet between us
It will never lose its character
It will destroy all barriers

Free

I have hidden your words in my scars
There are too many scars
The scars have names
Scars from every time you hit me
Beat me, cussed at me and hurt me
One time, you called me a whore, so the one on my heart
    is named
that
One time, you put a chair on my foot, so that one is
    named chair
One time, you hit me with a wooden picture frame, so the
    one on my
hand is named frame
I am not your training dummy from a self-defense class
The jabs and uppercuts have stopped hurting
Your kicks have lessened
You must stop choking me when I talk back
I gasp for air and you do not care
You aren't going to hurt me
You are not stable to begin with
I always knew that
If I took away your tools, you would be an unamused mule
My dreams are to be superior, magnificent, and free
I am free in my mind
free in my demeanor; I am a strong believer
The jeopardy of your soul
You can't even understand
It must be black and have little gray holes
Rotten and hanging like a thread
The spiders like it there; they've made it their bed
It is their home, where they love to roam and get fed

You cough a lot; detox your lungs
And clean out your heart
So that spider web can break apart
You may perhaps want to just die
You must be filthy
Spiders can smell your death
The decaying of your arms, the blackening of your feet
Seem to be a rash or life being swept away, don't you think?
To the spiders, it is the trash they yearn for
I hope you don't rot to death
That might be best
But you may not have eternal rest
You never let me rest
But I wish you the best
You see the police are on the way
You will pay for everything you ever did to me
I don't have any regrets

They say

They say black lives matter
I wish they acted like it was true Society claims black
    women are angry
Well, I am a black woman
People who are not black don't understand
Yes, they know pain, but they could care less about
    my name
White people call me Veronica, but clearly, there is no r, o,
    c, or n in my name
My name is Vatekia. They say, "Oh, that is close enough.
How about I call you Tamia instead of Tangela?"
They say some blacks are illiterate
Well, some of them don't know how to read a name
You say, "I don't want to butcher your name."
But you are silent when they butcher "Blacks" every day
You are not helping them; you remain quiet
Quiet does not stop us from dying
What if your brother was lying on the ground, screaming
    for his mom while being suffocated?
Blacks were not angry until now because you don't value us
When we started making these products that you use
    before you existed
If your daughter was killed in her sleep from a bullet
Wouldn't you weep? Wouldn't you want justice?
Why settle when you do not get the justice you deserve?
Well, that is how we feel as Blacks So, before you say all
    lives matter
Just think of all the sacrifices Blacks have made for
    this world
If you don't support us We won't support you
We have businesses and dues too

We are tired of being abused and kicked, swept away and
    tossed to the side
Like old dirt on the steps
Right is right and wrong is wrong
Humans are created in God's image, all of us
But you turn your back on us
We caused you no harm
We are not scary looking; we are humans too
We are not threatening
Stop calling the police on us You call them for nothing This
    is getting insane We are not to blame
We walk peacefully through a neighborhood and get shot
We are unarmed, minding our own business
You played with us in school and shared your toys
    and games
We cried together, laughed together, and even held hands
Sung Ring Around the Rosie and Sticks and Stones
Now you don't want to stand with us
It makes me sad
Now some of y'all can't be trusted
This world is getting divided The devil is walking around and
You have the nerve to hold his hand
You want to help now
It might be too late now
Well, just come join the crowd and make us Blacks proud
A change must come soon
Or maybe God will just burst through the sky, disap-
    pointed, and just cry

Broken promises

There is a little boy on the step. He hasn't moved in two hours. He is just sitting there, crying. He had called his dad, who never answered. His mom told him his dad would be there by 2 pm; it is 4 pm now. Broken promises should not be what he is becoming used to. Cries at night; cries at school on family days. "Mommy, Joshua's dad came to school today. Why didn't my dad show up?" "I don't know. Maybe he got called in for work this time. I'm sorry, baby." The little boy likes to draw and ride his bike. He draws pictures of his dad and mom holding hands and him playing. He talks about his dad to his friends as if he did no wrong. To him, his dad was an angel without wings. His mom cries at night, praying for his dad to come around. His dad hasn't been around in eight months. She is drained from the responsibilities of being a single parent. Late nights at work, lack of sleep, packing lunches, cleaning, and driving. Bleeding, stomach cramps, peeing every five minutes, and pelvic pain. She had signed up for this, but then again, she had not. It takes two to tie loose ends. She thought they had a mutual understanding. She let his dad kick it and romance her when they were not on solid terms. She said it wouldn't hurt, but before she knew it, she was hurt. Her belly was growing like a watermelon—big, round, and striped with dark lines. Nauseous, throwing up after every meal, and head spinning like a fan. She knew she was not pretending. This was just the beginning. He told her he loved her and wanted her but got married to another woman the next day. She was so oblivious to that union. She gives her son everything he ever longed for besides his dad. She can't make her son's father a man. Now, it is her mission to never fall in love with a person so lame. She said, "It is such a shame. Love should never be played like a game." She can't run when life does not go her way. She can't run away when her son needs new shoes or when he needs his diaper changed. I am all for women empowerment. You can be an independent woman, but who wants to one hundred percent of the time? Women can get tired too, just like men, while caring for children and pets. Let him contribute; ask him for what you want. Tell him to watch the children while you go to the spa and just take time for yourself. You already have one child. You don't need or want him acting like a child too. Someone had raised him already; it may not have been his mother, but someone did. If he had raised himself, then, I hope it has not made him insane. There are ways around schedules. Some men don't deserve to have rights to their kids or their kid's last name. She carried the child; he came out of her. I wish men could carry children too. Things would not be the same; their life would change. So, here's a shout out and good vibes to the men who take care of their children. So, shout out to the women who suffer in silence though all this could have been prevented if you had used your brain and thought logically. Don't let people fill your head with lies and leave you confused and feeling abused. Start building real relationships with strings attached. He never paid his debt to you, and you let him use you for a roof over his head and for sex. You knew what he was and how he acted before you let him get a piece of you so do not complain now. You knew he lied first before you were pregnant. You knew he was a flirt. You knew you were not the only person he texted and called. You knew he talked smoothly. You knew he was a romancer. Did you think you could make him different? Did he say you were his one and only? Don't fall for that player's lines.

He will owe you more and leave you as quickly as he makes you experience a physical sensation. Would you rather endure suffering, penetration, and wrinkles? Would you want to deprive your children a lot of what you had growing up? Do you want your children to experience birthdays and important events without their parents? Do you want to keep depending on welfare your whole life? Why do you want debt? Don't you want better for yourself? If you get married, at least you can say you tried to help the situation. Please stay away from him if he hits you or abuses you in any form. Don't hurt your kids with images of betrayal. He broke your heart, so you just abandon your kids because they look like him and not you. Every time you look at your son, you see his father's face. I understand it is not fair being alone or left behind. You used to be in love with him and now you can't stand him. What changed? What woman did you see him with? What did she say to you? It does not matter unless he is dangerous. That was three years ago; let stuff go. Get to know his wife for the sake of the child. You constantly bash him, but he apologized and tried to help. You tell him you don't need his wealth, and you tell him he is not good for anything. Why do you call his wife names when she feeds your child and combs his hair to help him out? I don't blame some of these males because some of these women are just as confused. You trusted him too much. Whose fault was that? You never looked behind your back. You looked for love and attention in the wrong place. I am sorry you had a rough life, but don't let being a former victim define you. Despite whatever happened, you survived it. That man is not your lifeline. Why do you depend on the government for money? I can understand if you don't have family or others to help, but some people just collect and can do better but don't. You should not care about extra tax money from having multiple babies. Your kids are your responsibility. Do you want a lifetime of happiness with tranquility, respect, reassurance, structure in the home, marriage, and love—and did I mention no regrets?

Sleep: A story of a girl

Sleep is her favorite hobby. Sleep is when no one bothers her. When she is awake, she is cold in the dark. Her fingers are not cold, but they are numb. Why? Her mom beats her hands until they sting, and they become numb and fragile. Her hands are calloused like from holding a rope for too long. Her punishment was to hold a broomstick for 40 minutes because she fell on her mom's dog and it died. She fell in the first place because her mom had pushed her. Her mom found her sneaking out of the house at 3 am two nights in a row. The girl's name is Jenna. She is only 16 years old, just a teenager, but she feels 26. Her back is deeply wounded as if a pitchfork had been dug into her skin for 10 minutes. Her mom was the devil in her eyes with eyes red as a red apple in a tree. Tall, muscular, and black, her dad stood at the door knocking. Her mom was white; her mom lived with the regret of having her. Jenna's maternal grandmother was white and racist. Her aggressive mom had beaten her for dating a black man in the past.

Jenna rushed to the door crying. Her dad said, "Jenna, what's wrong?" She replied, "Nothing! I am just so happy that you are here." The mom said, "That is great, honey. See you tomorrow. I love you." The daughter picked up her backpack and said, "I love you too." When the father and daughter got home, he took her backpack off and saw the scars on her neck. "How did this happen?" "I am not sure, Dad." Her head in her lap, she shed tears as she said, "Mom did it, Dad. She told me not to tell you. She is so mean to me. Look!" Then Dad said, "Baby, you are not going back to her anymore, okay? This is serious and it's child endangerment." She softly mumbled, "Ok. Please, Dad, save me from her! She told me I am ugly and that I would never be beautiful even if I used makeup. She said no man would want me as a wife when I get older because of the gap in my teeth. I sleep a lot over there so that she will leave me alone, but sometimes, she comes in and pours cinnamon, vinegar, and lemon juice on me. The lemon juice burns my eyes so bad, Dad!" "Jenna, let me take pictures of you, honey, and let's go to the police. You are very beautiful, and anyone who thinks differently is a fool," said Dad. "Thanks, Dad. Sleep is my way to be free from her, Dad. She is a monster. Sleep should not be so much fun. I am just a kid."

Gradually, she reduced the time spent on her old favorite pastime and basketball became her favorite hobby. Sleep is okay, but now, her mission is to be happy and to play outside more like a normal kid. Her spirit was enriched with tranquility and confidence. Her dad was her hero. She wore tiaras, participated in fashion shows, and became the junior pageant winner. Jenna graduated college with a degree in criminal justice. Jenna is 25 years old now and is a family defense lawyer for child victims of crimes. She wants to protect innocent kids because she knows the anguish and physical and emotional pain she experienced as a kid. I met Jenna last year. She is also a public speaker now. Another fun fact, she has a husband who is as sweet to her as honey. She is currently pregnant with her first child. Jenna vowed to always be loving to her children and to make sure she protects them from predators like her mom. Jenna's mom is currently serving 25 years in prison, and she writes Jenna letters once a month to apologize and tell her that she is proud of her. Jenna sees a therapist every three months just to make sure she is on the right path because, sometimes, victims can develop bad habits like experimenting with drugs to help them deal with the pain from the abuse. Jenna still experiences nightmares sometimes. Jenna's husband is very supportive and rubs her back at night so she can feel calm. Her husband is her best friend.

Blue

Somber skies and twisted streams
These sights give me a sense of meaning
The tulips tall as the storks in the barn
You may know my name
But you sure don't know my voyage
Black rooms but with light available
Blue as the sky you seem to beam
Blue is you; blue is me
Blue is the pretty bird up in the tree
Blue is confidence, stability, and wisdom
Elegance and calmness
I don't know why people say they are feeling blue
To me, blue is great
If I feel blue, it means I feel great
Just like the day we met
Your favorite color is midnight blue
My favorite color is surf blue
Years ago, at driving school, I saw a surf Blue PT Cruiser
That was a cool driving school
Ever since that day, surf blue has been my favorite color
Sweet blue memories
If I could have everything blue, I would
I had blue glasses before, I had a blue phone, I had a blue
     watch, need
I say more?
Blue is my smile
Blue is my heart
Blue is the ring that gives off a spark
Blue gave me a reason to start seeing you
My heart was blue when you arrived at the door
Blue is the way I'll feel about you forever more

A Story of a Troubled Woman

The joy of being a mother, her friend, Trish, will never know. Trish is married to a man, and she has fertility issues. While her friend, Ms. Josie Losin, goes to entertain males and have casual flings, her child is home alone and, he needs his father in his life. Sometimes Josie's son is watched by Trish. She tells her friend not to stay out so late. However, in vain to her lectures, Josie says back off. Trish said, "I might be the one you call, but the child is yours; you are on your own. I will no longer watch him at night because of your greed. Here I am struggling to have a child and you are so quick to leave yours. I go to the fertility clinic every three months. I feel like I am cheating my husband because of this issue. I am a woman who can't seem to have children and you know this." The next day, Josie's son was riding a bike to school and a truck hit him. He flew into the air and plummeted to the ground. The ambulance paramedics staff said it didn't look good. The mom got a call from the school and then the hospital. "Hello, Ms. Losin, please get down here quick. Your son, Daniel, was in a terrible accident." "Okay, I am on my way." With silence, sighs, and cries, Ms. Losin grabbed her keys and sprinted out of the house door. If anything happens to him. God help me, help us please. Ms. Losin called her best friend, Trish, who came to pick her up and drive her to the hospital. They got to the hospital to find her son in a coma. "He is only eight years old and a good kid. Why him?" cried out his mom. Trish said, "Yes, honey, he is. And I wish you had spent more time with him. He needs you there more often. I am so sorry about this. The driver should have not been speeding." Ms. Losin replied, "God, I'll do anything; just let my son live. I will stop going out so much. Please make my baby improve and strengthen him. I don't know what I would do without him, Jesus!" Ms. Losin and Trish stayed at the hospital all night. Trish had to go to work the next night, so she went home. Ms. Losin stayed by her son's side for a week before her manager from work called and asked her if she was coming back. She said, "please give me 2–3 more days and I will be back. I will call my son's dad to see if he can help." Her manager, Sharena, said, "Sure, whatever you need. Please know that we care about you and are praying for you and your family." "Thanks, Sharena." Weeks went by without any improvement in Daniel. Then, Josie finally called Johan, Daniel's dad. The phone rang and he answered, "Hello, Josie?" Is that you?" Speaking softly with a crack in her voice, she said, "Yes, Johan." "You sound like you are crying." "Umm, I called because our baby is in the Calvert Darlington Hospital. You need to get here now. Johan, our baby, he can't talk. I need help with him." "Josie, just breath and I will be there in 20 minutes, okay?" "Okay, goodbye," said Josie. Trish called Josie to ask her if she was hungry. "Girl, yes, please bring me some food. This hospital food is nasty." Trish replied, "Girl, you don't have to tell me, I know!" Johan arrived at the front desk and asked to see his son. The nurse escorted him to the room. Johan entered the room and burst out crying. "Don't act like you are sad now. You are full of shit, Johan, acting all concerned. You need to do your part. You should have been doing your part. Where is your ugly wife, huh? Does she even know you have a child?" Johan wiped her tears and gave her a hug and just held her and kissed her. "What was that for? Are you crazy?" asked Josie. "I have been doing a lot of thinking. Yes, my ex-wife knew I had a child, but that is over. We got divorced last year, and I live alone now. She was screwing my best friend and lied about it. Josie, I am sorry about the way we ended it, but I would like to repair our relationship. I was young when you were pregnant, and we had our son. I was a player. I looked for love in the wrong places when it was right in front of me. I am mature now. I know what I want now." Josie laughed, clapped, and said, "Cut! Get off stage, stop fronting! I let you kiss me because I was vulnerable. Don't play me for a fool, boy!" "I'm serious, Josie. All I want is you! Let me take you out on a date like we used to do. How about Thursday after work, and then, we can come here to see our son?" "Josie responded, I guess that would be okay. It's just a date. Don't try anything!" "Great, what did the doctor say about our son?" asked Johan. "He is stable now but not breathing on his own yet. He has a breathing tube in his throat, and he gets his food through this IV here. See, it's the yellow, green, and clear one. He has a tube in his butt that collects his stool as well and a urinary catheter in his private area. This is so sad, but we will get through it. They said he can hear us talk." said Josie. "Daddy is here, Son. I love you, and I can't wait until we can play football in the yard. Would you like that, Son? I want you and your mom to move in with me so I can help her with you. She is so strong, and you are too. I didn't realize a good thing when I had it. Just rest champ," said Johan. He rubbed Josie's arms and shoulder and then sat down very close beside her in a chair. Josie and Johan went home that day and visited their son together every day. About 20 days later, when Johan and Josie entered the room, they saw Daniel moving and Josie screamed for a nurse, "Oh my God! He's moving! Nurse, Nurse, hurry! Daniel moved his fingers." The nurse, Sirtin, said, "That might be good news. Sometimes comma patients move from a nervous system trigger." She checked his pupils and vitals. "Nothing has changed, Ms. Losin. I'm sorry." The nurse left the room. Josie sighed. Josie and Johan held their son's hand. "Daniel, if you can hear my voice, bend your finger again two times." Daniel did not bend his finger, but five hours later, he did. Two hours after that, he opened his eyes and whispered, "Dad? I love you too. I heard you say that you can't wait until we can play foot-ball in the yard." Johan screamed, "Nurse Sirtin, Josie was right. He is improving. He is awake now and talking." Nurse Sirtin heard him from her desk, rushed in and said, "Well, I'll be darned. This is a first for me. I'm surprised and I'm so happy for you and your wife." Johan replied, "Well, she is not my wife, but I hope we can work on that." "You could have fooled me the way you two have been looking at each other. You better marry her. You two look good together and your boy needs a big support system." Johan said, "Yes, I agree." Josie gave her keys to Johan so he could start moving her belongings to his house and they could live together. "Baby boy, Daddy will be back. I'm going to move you and your mommy's things to my house." "Yay! I've dreamed about this happening. I love you guys!" "I love you too" declared Johan. "I love you, baby," said Josie. Trish walked into the room and stopped in her tracks. "Wow, you are awake, sweetie! Daniel, oh my God! God is so good. Girl, you need to start going to church with me. This is a miracle. You too, Johan." Trish laughed and hugged Daniel. Two months later, Daniel arrived at his new house with his family. His parents got married the next week and Josie found out she was preg-nant again but, this time, with a girl. Trish helped them decorate the house. "Don't worry, Trish. I'm not going out leaving my children at night anymore. I am married now, and I have learned my lesson. Mrs. Jans sounds good, doesn't it? Daniel will be such a good big brother and Johan is a changed man, girl. Who would have thought?" Johan and Josie sat in the lounge chairs in the backyard, watching Daniel as he swam in the pool. Johan kissed and rubbed Josie's stomach and said, "I love you, Mrs. Jans." "I love you more, Mr. Jans," uttered Josie. Later, Trish gave Josie a small pink gift bag and told her to look inside. Josie unwrapped the pink wrapping paper in the fragile bag and saw a baby shirt that read 'The best auntie ever.' Josie yelled, "What!" "Yeah, I'm pregnant with a girl," Trish said excitedly. Josie got up and hugged her friend. "Congratulations! Our kids will have so much fun together. Why didn't you tell me?" "You were going through a tough time and I wanted to wait until things got better," replied Trish. Josie answered, "Aww, I understand." The happy family received so many gifts. Trish and her husband were overjoyed by the upcoming new edition.

Desires

We were in the same boat on the sea by the dark horizon until that sweet day. When we met on that fateful day, it was like stars bursting through the darkness. What a beautiful setting! When I think of you, I don't want to stop the daydreams. I heard you are a dreamer. I heard you are a sweetheart, but you can make smart remarks too from time to time. I can make smart remarks too, so it's cool. It will be like fireworks without the harsh sounds. When our hands touch, it will be like rubbing a lap dog's bushy head. The aroma of your soul is cinnamon with coconut drizzled on the top layer of your heart which beats rapidly like how the warm filled crumps fall. When it beats, it leaves a mark. Your arms are my shield, and you hold me in the dark. You say, "Don't worry, it's just thunder, and it's just about to start again." The essence of your trauma is not understood, but such is life; you must go on. I wish I could erase your bad memories, but it made you stronger and better at being my tailor-made lover. When God made you, maybe he drew you near me, made a maze, and told you where to go to find me when you got older. He let the past lovers go because they never understood your lifestyle. They cared for your money and not you. They fell in love with potential. Well, I fell in love with your charming voice and your mindset of wanting more and putting in the work. You told me that God has a plan for our lives. You made it your mission to pursue your dreams and asked me if that was what I wanted as well. You asked me about my dreams and offered a helping hand. God knew I could fit in your schedule someday. God loves us so much that he took the time to keep us apart until we got older so we could know how to love and realize our trials and errors before entering a union. So yes, we are still in the same boat. I am still yours, and that won't change. Who said you can't have your cake and eat it too? I can and I believe you can as well. There will be turmoil, but we will get through it. Please understand that if I've loved you this long, I will love you forever and a day. I have loved you through every season and for many reasons. I don't have any reason to stop loving you, and don't give me a reason. Our love has extended past the seasons, past a year, and it will last forever. You gave me a reason to keep dreaming, to keep breathing, to keep fighting, to keep believing, and to keep achieving. Our love is strengthened by God, so I thank him for that investment he made in us. I found a prize when I looked into your eyes. I found everything I desired when I took that first chance, that first glance, and that first dance with you. We were in the same boat and we still are in the same boat. I wonder where the current will take us next! We will explore many chapters in our lives. I heard you were a dreamer. Well, now your dream is coming true.

The Story of Maria and her Family

The bird sits and waits for the sun. Grant kissed her lips and said, "I love you, Hun." His lips spoke deceit, but he hid it with his smile. The momentum of his strength made her sing. "Where is your ring?" he asked. The pace of her speech slowed. "I'm sorry, love. I took it off to cook." With her hands wrinkled like two dried apples, she cut some fruit for a snack. Their kids ate like cavemen. Her breasts seemed heavier and sagged like a sack of potatoes. Her husband noticed. "Babe, your boobs look heavier. Are you pregnant?" Maria softly replied, "I don't know, babe. Let's check. I have a test in the purse under my desk." She took the test to the bathroom and sat on the toilet, sweating as if she were in a sauna heat room. Grant went to check on the boys who were on the sofa. The boys were playing Mario Kart. "You're stupid, Luigi," yelled Joseph. His brother, Wyatt, shouted, "Yeah, take that!" They both laughed. Rich, the dog, jumped on the sofa. "Ouch, Rich you hurt me!" Rich was a three-year-old Golden Retriever. "I'm done playing now. The last one to get to the playroom stinks!" said Wyatt. He turned off the TV, and they both ran up the stairs. Grant came out of the bathroom, went to the porch and cried. Maria followed Grant to the porch. "Babe, I love you and the baby, but we are at our wit's end financially. I"ll start looking for a second job to work in the evenings. It will be alright, honey." Maria cried and said, "It will be alright, Grant. We will be great, and Ms. Tarsun from my job gave me a raise a month ago. It's right on time! Baby, I know you've been seeing another woman, so maybe we should separate before the baby gets here." Grant looked crestfallen at this statement. Grant said, "Baby, I am so sorry. I wanted to tell you. I did not want you to find out like this. It's over now anyway. I told her you're pregnant and that I'm never going to see her again." "The audacity of you to lie to my face!" Maria replied through tears. "She called me this morning. I will raise this baby on my own. Go pack your bags and get out of this house. She told me you told her you were going to see her tonight. However, you told me you were working late tonight. You have no respect for this family." Grant packed his bags to leave. Soon, Giselle came to the house to talk to Maria and Grant. Maria was devastated. "Grant, you told this tramp where we live! You must have lost your mind!" Giselle face turned red and she looked furious. Giselle spoke to Maria, "I am so sorry. He told me he was single, believe me. I know you are upset but please don't call me a tramp. Ever since I've known he's married; he won't have me either. This is trifling!" "We have been having financial problems, but cheating is not what he should have done. I've been a good wife to him. He destroyed my family, and I just found out I'm pregnant with his baby, said Maria." Giselle said, "Here, take my number if you want to talk more and congratulations on the baby." Giselle wrote down her number on a piece of paper and gave it to Maria. "Thank you goodbye," replied Maria. Giselle got into her car and left. Maria saw Grant, slapped him and yelled, "How dare you! We are done. You can pick up your other belongings in the morning." Grant sighed and looked sorrowful. Grant said, "I used to go to the club to relax at night. That's where I met her. She was a dancer, and one thing lead to another. I was drunk, babe. We had sex every night for about two weeks and that's it." He drove off and came back only two months later. Maria had told the kids he was on a work trip. When he came back, everything returned to normal. Maria took him back because he seemed to be a changed man. He had a new job and he moved the family to a big mansion. Maria warned Grant, "Babe, if you pull that again, I will gut you like a fish. I mean it." "I've learned my lesson, Maria. Home is with you forever. We are adding another blessing here soon and I should have never left. I was such a fool." Maria said, "Yes, your head got too big." They both laughed and their love for one another blossomed with each day.

More

I don't have feelings for you
The more I talked to you
The more I saw your face
The attractiveness of your face turned my mind to think
How I loved seeing your face
The more I heard your voice, it sounded calming and happy
The more I held your hand, it felt comfortable to me
The more dates we went on, it was fun to be out with a male,
To eat and laugh
No, it was not love
Love lasts
Love doesn't make you feel uncomfortable
Love is easy
If it were love, you wouldn't have to beg
I was not pleased
You weren't pleasing
After the blink of an eye
I didn't like your teasing of others
I couldn't stand looking at your face
I was disgusted at the thought of you
Your voice became dry and ugly to me
Whiny like a little girl with an attitude
You did not want space, yet I did
Your cries were pathetic
You made your bed, now go lay in it
I don't feel sorry for you

You thought you knew everything
But you didn't know how to keep a woman
You didn't know what to say or how to say it
You didn't care to fix that aspect
You need to grow up and stop trying to be
Mister take charge of everything

I Love You Forever

I love you forever and always
On our wedding night, you said I made you feel tingles all
    down your spine
The art of your arch
The assignment of your yoga
The skeleton I used to see left when we met
You have brightened; your veins are noticeable
You have become proficient and are eager to learn
Your ambience is a halo
Your smile lights up the mood of those near you
You don't even notice the effect you have on me and others
    until I tell you
You brighten up my heart every day that I see your face
    and hear your voice

<u>If I had</u>

If I got a rose every time I thought of you, I'd have the biggest garden you could imagine.

The forte of your gifts, the repetitive measures of your melodies, and the crescendo of your pauses.

I know you are a gift. You display many gifts to me and to the world.

His Russian hat. The pruning of his feet. Good grief!

He liked to peek at the noise outside.

He liked to watch the middle aspect of his globe; it had a picture of his ex-wife that brought him poor memories.

He didn't want to go on when the hurt set in, but he is fine now.

His interest has turned to being in love with a woman from North Dakota, and she lights his fire.

Karina is her name, and she is his gain.

Flexibility is her craft and her classiness is felt from a performance.

She is a gymnast of her own kind. She tells him how to stand, how to pose, and how to get above and below the belt to avoid sprains, aches, and pains.

If I had more delicate illusions, I would grab a paint brush and go work near the ocean on a rock in the mountains or a tall cliff to try to paint the way I feel about you. As high as a tower, that's the way you make me feel.

You give me a natural, calming vibe, and that is what you mean to me—you make me free and live without regrets.

News

Please shed a tear if you feel like it is needed. Please shed tears of joy if you want to. Please don't shed tears because of a person who does not deserve you. Please don't listen to others' opinions unless you know they are positively inspired. Release the pain. Release the burden. Release the fear of being hurt. Release the fear of voicing your opinion. Save the speech on your dreams for someone who cares. Don't tell your plans to the snake you call a friend or family member. Your eyes are blue, but they are red when you scream and are mean. Please don't apologize, it may be too late. Family is family but that doesn't mean they are rooting for you. Any person can hide behind a smile and compliment. They may even throw dirt on your name, lie and try to manipulate. They laugh at you behind closed doors. They call you beautiful to your face, and while alone, they call you fat, skinny, ugly, dumb and they say it is sad. You should have lived with your dad. The list goes on. Who made you the queen or king of judgement? No one. Ever since we have existed, I have never witnessed you receive an award with this honor. You don't sit high, you sit low. No one needs an explanation. You don't need validation. You don't need approval. Refusal is normal too. I am sorry you went through that but what is mine is not yours. I will not let you suck the life out of me like she did to you. You should have left her and them at the door. Should have entrapped their spirit in your home. Chaos and yeast grow on your walls. They have left a mark like danger signs and cones. Scattered pieces, they are missing a link. She even left a trail by the sink. Don't ask her to clean up, she reeks. A whiff, oh please! She walks like she has five sharpies up her ass and so does that man. When she laughs, poison comes out of her mouth, but she is aware. Don't sit and stare at the glares and chains. Get out! She needs to change. You said, "I am cold." I said, "I am awake. I am present and when I last checked, you weren't a supernatural ruler." I am wise for my years. I am aware of my surroundings. I am aware that you weren't grounded. Your mind was scattered, beaten, and I told you it didn't matter because it doesn't matter; it was a lesson learned. You could have screamed louder, but it wouldn't matter because you are damaged goods. The repair you need is far more than I was led to see and informed of. So, it doesn't matter because you don't fit in my life peacefully. I don't want any parts of you. I would have been your next victim, but I saw through you before we made the headlines. I didn't have a clue that you were this silly and bruised.

My Honey

Roses are red, but why can't they be blue?
Why are bricks brown when they are as solid as gold?
Why is honey so good yet so messy and sticky?
My honey is a smile ever so bright
When I looked into his eyes, I noticed a hole
A hole and a story behind them
A hole that needed to be filled
Who has holes that need to be filled?
Many honeys do
Rivers are blue, but I love the moon
The moon is ever so calming yet deceptive
Deceptive like his eyes and mouth
Wisconsin would be magnificent if it was more diverse
I love cheese and so does my mother
Idaho might be ruling if they were known for fried chicken
    and not potatoes
Marvelous as the sun, we glowed when we touched
Please don't rush
His skin was like a baby's face
Feet just like sand
I knew the sun was going down soon
I knew the cars would halt
I knew his heart was strong and had a spark
But why do we never go to a park?
To bring back sparks
Why hide in the dark?
How about we go back to the start
When his soul was hungry for more
His tongue spoke truth and diligence
His disposition was different
I am glad we positioned

Roses are red, but why can't they be blue?
Maybe because
God is good and his blood was red
Red is what keeps us together
My honey is a smile ever so bright
Now can we make things right?

Love

They say love is a waste of time
But is it a waste for my mind to think?
About you all day?
My heart sings when you are around
Love is not a waste of time It gives you more time to live
More opportunities to smile
More reasons to find time to go out with someone
Who said love is a waste of time?
I would like to look inside their mind
I can't but I would try to hear their thoughts
Their trials and errors and their devotion
And what their hurt was
That was lust and wrongdoings and not love
Clearly, they don't know what love is
Because the person wasn't displaying it
Love doesn't hurt, it heals
Love doesn't punch or stab, it feels softly
And gently without aggression, force, or manipulation
Love is the greatest of all That's why I chose it
Love is not a waste of time Feel free to ask me why

All this time

All this time
I have been loving you
All this time
You have been loving me
If you pull this again, we are through
But you are good for my heart
I know
Ever since you have been in my life
There is sunshine in my being
I want to spend my life with you
I want to grow old with you
All this time
You gave me a reason to smile
I laugh when I think of us
Fun times, dark times, all my times with you
Are what I am blessed with
I know that I have found someone worth fighting for
I know that I have found someone worth dying for
I knew when I first saw your face
That you were filled with grace
You passed the exam and aced it
All this time, I have been studying you
You have studied me well too
Strokes of a pencil glide on a paper as I write
The pencil has been sharpened about five times
That is how much I can write about you
And baby, I never get tired
Serendipity is our motive
Philosophy is our outlet
To be honest, you are everything
I have ever wanted in a man

Fear of God, humor, creativity, and charm
Just to name a few because I have over 22 reasons why I love you
I don't want your head to swell, baby
That would not be a pretty scene
I would tell the director "cut" and "don't tape this"
He would be mean
You are never mean to me though
And this isn't a dream anymore
All this time, I have loved you
If I loved you for nine years, I will love you forever
When we grow fragile and weak, still the love will be there
All this time
And my love for you grows every day

<u>We are</u>

We are not who they say we are, we are who God says we are. If they had never said it, would it have mattered? God already told us that he paid the price for us. This coronavirus is taking a toll on us. If I can touch one person, my life would not be in vain. I want to encourage when it is hard to encourage. I want to bestow and speak life into you so your life may be touched. I have had many sleepless nights. I have had thoughts race through my mind. I have shed tears hoping for change in others and in the world. I have experienced heartbreak. I am here to tell you that you will live and get through it. God is preparing you for something greater. Eyes have not seen, and ears have not heard what is about to take place. Your destiny is God's plans for you. He knows your thoughts. He knows your heart. He knows the hairs on your head. He knows what makes you smile. He knows what makes you laugh. Think over your life. How have you made it this far? It was only by his grace. I am sure there were times you did not think you would see the next day, but you survived to see the next day. You are here for a reason because of his divine will. God will see to his plan so, don't fret when things don't go your way. I can tell you this from experience because companies act like they want you to have about 10 years of experience after graduating college and it is frustrating.

Advice

You said you won't take my advice because I am single. Well, did you ever ask why I am single? You would rather take advice from an 18-year-old chick who has 6 kids with 6 different baby daddies or a 40-year-old man with 5 kids and 3 different baby mommas? Why are the terms baby daddy so common? Why are the terms baby mama so common? Why do people think it is cool to say my baby momma or baby father is better than yours? That does not sound good. Why can't you make them your husband or wife? If you aren't married, even: saying that is my child's mom sounds better than a baby momma. If you don't have some respect for yourself, that's all you will ever be. You should set boundaries for men and women. They ignore your texts because they don't want you. Why can't you see that? They will send a text message saying "wyd Mami?" and could care less about your struggles for real. Just think before you act. It is not the man's fault all the time. I never liked the term. Why can't one say that's my son's father or daughter's father and vice versa? People have become accustomed to thinking that single parents who were never married should be glorified. I grew up believing only God should be glorified. Everyone is not meant to be married and that is completely fine. Hmm, am I in the wrong generation? My mom calls me an old woman, and I don't mind that. I have an old soul. I have style and charisma as well. You get mad when I give advice. You get married just to get divorced a year later. You call me rude. Now, who is not rude? People don't like to hear the truth.

You should have listened, and you wouldn't be crying. You said, "You didn't even sugarcoat it." Well, you should be scared to sugarcoat and lose that tooth of yours. That man might knock that tooth out for you for a bad reason. You have been warned—stay away from demons. They are not all pleasing.

Good things

They say all things must come to an end
And I stand torn but looking good on the outside
My insides are sad but lively Speckled with black holes
Is what it feels like
Rotten and molded but as red as a juicy watermelon
With white and black seeds
The heart has four chambers, but I feel like my heart has three
Ever since you went away
I have felt sad and confused
How can a person with so much laughter be gone?
I must not question the Creator
He knows what is best
Good things do come to an end but
My Savior has said, "The meek shall inherit the Earth."
He said, "The Lord is close to the broken hearted."
I can't live without God
The Great Jehovah, Messiah and my King
The Lord renews a right spirit within you.
The peace that comes with looking at the ocean and clouds
Is indescribable
So, imagine what Heaven is like They say all things come to an end
But after the Earth, good things will keep coming, not ending
Oh, I want to see his glorious face
We will live on forever where we will be free from sin

Her

Her throat is coated with flowers, lilies to be exact
She sang like it was her favorite song
She danced with poise, like the reflection of a rainbow
Scattered but precise and harmonious
Her smile looked if she had just been proposed to
Her voice as soft as a flute being played
I loved her
He loved her
But most of all
She loved her
She is I
She is me
She is victorious and a royal array
She walks with her head high
Her shoulders skyward
Thinking is love enough
Love is enough when we make it enough
Love is enough when we make it our guide
Love is enough when we hold ourselves accountable
She said, "I've never experienced a love like this."
It was there all along, she just didn't open the door
To be sure, she made a list of everything she wanted in a man
Love wasn't enough because she was not thinking of love
when she made the list
She was thinking of biases
Every guy is not the same
Every woman is not the same
Every smile is not in vain
Who is to blame for my pain?
I didn't give love a try
Isn't that a shame?

I am to blame
But when I meet him, what a change it will be
What will I change?
My last name but not anything else
I would stand in the rain to see him
Love won't let me be the same
It will make me change
I love her
She is a prize
She can't be tamed

Harmony's life

The torment in her soul
The desperation in her eyes
She wants this
But is she willing to take that dive?
Thunder rolls, hollow whistles at the shore
Clashing windows and, she forgot to pick up her crown
Her humbling spirit has hushed
Creatures say she is goody two shoes
They don't know she used to reckless
No one asked her if she was okay
Except for her boyfriend Drackir
His name has origins from a sphere
God is where serenity is present
She wishes life wasn't like this
She grew up in a foster home
Abused by the staff
But her boyfriend was there for her
every step of the way to protect her when he could
They were best friends
Until they got separated from the home
Around age 13 and, they met again and dated in high school.
Drackir is her hero
Her name is Harmony
However, her life was never peaceful,
He brought peace to her life and, she clung to him every
chance she could
She ran away and moved with him and, they agreed to
stick together:
No one knows what that poor girl endured,
She knows she can trust Drackir with her life,
Torment in her soul

Emptiness, trust issues, confusion
All because of some staff members
Who were supposed to help and teach her but did the opposite?
It's a cold world but, karma is evident.
She is healing
She is wise
Her heart will be free to sing,
Harmony and Drackir are well on their way to be the next big producers in the industry;
She is a sapphire
Always standing-out beautifully
She is a dream come true for Drackir
He couldn't wait any longer to ask,
"Will you marry me, Harmony?"
Harmony shouted, "A million times yes, baby!"
I want to spend the rest of my life with you. You are my heart and my world. I can't see myself with anyone else!

Vatekia's Mission

I picked the title "The Charms of Honey Chronicles" because I feel like I have a calling to write creatively and encourage others. I enjoy showcasing art. People require words, emotions, and reassurance. The world is not alright right now. I feel like we all need Jesus now more than ever before. If you don't believe in Jesus, then I will pray for you. Once, I asked a guy if he attended church. He told me, "I am black, of course." I was puzzled but I said, "Oh ok." I thought, what does being black have to do with who you worship? Anyway, I want to help single parents by getting them to think before they take life-altering decisions. I want people to think about the big picture and not what is in front of them at the moment. Change is needed. I seek deliverance in souls. Atmospheres, libraries, arenas, and stadiums should be filled for good causes. The funny part about me being an author is that I was an avid reader in elementary school, but after that, I stopped enjoying it. I am picky about what I read. If something doesn't interest me, I won't read it. It wasn't until I took a creative writing class in tenth grade that I got serious about memoirs, poems, plays, and so on. The year before that, in ninth grade, I was a semi-finalist in a poetry contest. I have grown so much since high school. Back to my title choice, "The Charms of Honey Chronicles" was about another thought I had. I thought about passion; honey is sweet and sticky, just like love. Love will make you do things you wouldn't normally do, and there would be bad times as well. You can choose honey and be willing to go through hard times when you are in love. I love honey in my tea, and I love charms. Charms are captivating and lovely, and most of my poems are about love. "Chronicles" just sounds cool and adventurous, like a journey. Life is a journey, and we all have obstacles to overcome. Poetry is a journey. I imagine the scenes as I write—the pauses, triumphs, hurt, expressions. I wanted to write about important issues and let people know that they are not alone. Millions of people have fertility issues like my character Trish. Many people have relationship issues; they take their cheating partners back and get judged by others, like Maria. Many people have been called unpleasant names. Many people are in their sixties but act sixteen when it comes to relationships, playing games and sleeping around, and it is not right or fair to the other parties. A ridiculous number of people have been told to keep their mouths shut about rape and abuse, no matter what the form. The truth will be revealed, and I hope God has mercy on our souls and this world. Mental health issues are on the rise, especially due to COVID-19. We are all breathing the same air. We must share and show concern. What does your reflection say? It shouldn't be *I am better than her, look at her shoes or I am taking all the bread off the shelf just because I can.* Greed is not love. Why should we kill our brothers and sisters, thinking we are invincible? We must strive to make life sweet as honey as we can make it!